DATE DUE

JUL 2 6 1977		
NOV 0 1 1977		
MAY 5 3 1978		
NO 17 '90		
JY 14 '92		
MAR 0 4 '95		
AN 27 '97		
DE 07 '99		

Other books for young readers

by the same author

Sir William and the Wolf

Havelok *and* Sir Orfeo

Crusader King

The Days of Chivalry

Sea-dogs and Pilgrim Fathers

A Picture History of India

With E. S. Harley

Books, from Papyrus to Paperback

The
House of Cats
&
Other Stories

———◆◎◆———

by JOHN HAMPDEN

illustrated by ENRICO ARNO

Farrar, Straus & Giroux · *New York*
An Ariel Book

*For
Charlotte
and
Catherine*

CONTENTS

The
House of Cats
&
Other Stories

1

The House of Cats

THERE was a time long ago when the animal people could talk, just like human people, and some of them were rich and some were poor, just like human people.

In these days there was a poor widow living in Tuscany who had two daughters. One of them was very good and pretty and the other was wicked and ugly. The pretty one, whose name was Lisina, went into the town to look for work, and she found it in a house full of cats, who were quite rich. She worked very hard for them, cooking the meals, making the beds, cleaning the floors, and polishing the furniture, and all the cats grew fond of her.

Presently the Great Cat, the father of them all,

came home. He had been on a journey to see his friends in another town.

"Has Lisina served you well?" he asked the little cats.

"Oh, yes," they answered, "she has worked very well, and she has been kind and helpful to us all."

Then the Great Cat, who was called the Gatto Mammone, led Lisina into a room where there were two very large, tall earthenware jars.

"Now," he said, "one of these jars is full of oil, and the other is full of gold. I am going to dip you into one of them. Which shall it be?"

Lisina thought hard for a minute, and thought it would be greedy to choose the gold, so she answered, "The oil, if you please, sir."

"No," said the Great Cat, "you have served us too well for that."

He picked her up very gently and dipped her into the jar full of gold. When he lifted her out, she was gilded from tip to toe.

Then the Great Cat said, "Now I will give you your wages and you can go home. You will hear the cock crow, and you must turn toward him, but when you hear the donkey bray you must turn away from him."

Lisina went home to her mother's cottage. As soon

as the cock saw her coming, he crowed lustily. She turned toward him, and at once a beautiful golden star grew out of her forehead. At that the donkey in the yard lifted his head and brayed at her, but she turned her back on him and went into the cottage.

You can just imagine how astonished her mother and sister were when they saw her gilded from head to foot, with a beautiful golden star growing out of her forehead. She told them her story, and at once the bad sister said, "*I* will go and work in the House of Cats."

Off she went to the town. The Great Cat had gone on his travels again, but the little cats took her in and set her to work. They soon found she was as wicked and lazy as she was ugly. She cooked them poor meals, she left the beds unmade, she swept the dust under the furniture, and she beat the kittens cruelly if they got in her way.

Fortunately the Great Cat soon came home. When he had heard their sad story, he took the girl into the room where the two jars were, and said, "One of these jars is full of oil, and the other is full of gold. I am going to dip you into one of them. Which shall it be?"

"The jar of gold, of course," said the ugly sister.

"Ah," said the Great Cat. "What a bad girl you are!"

5

He dipped her into the oil, and then he rolled her in the kitchen cinders so that they stuck all over her.

"Now," said the Great Cat. "Off with you! And when you hear the donkey bray, turn toward him."

The bad girl ran off. When the donkey saw her coming, he brayed loud and long, she turned to face him, and immediately a donkey's tail grew out of her forehead and stood bolt upright on her head.

When the mother saw the state her favorite daughter was in, she was very angry with the pretty sister, and told her that she was the cause of it all. She dragged Lisina into her bedroom and locked her in. The girl sat there at her bedroom window knitting, and it happened that the Prince came riding by on his favorite pony. He looked at her, gilded as she was, with a golden star growing out of her forehead, and he thought her the most beautiful girl he had ever seen. She looked at him in his fine clothes, and thought him the most handsome young man in the world.

Slipping from his saddle and doffing his hat, he bowed low to her, and said, "Fair maiden, will you marry me?"

"Oh, sir," she cried, "I will!"

"Then I will go back to my palace and bring my carriage to fetch you," said he.

But Lisina's mother had heard all this. As soon as the Prince had ridden away, she took the pretty sister and locked her in a cupboard. Then she dressed the bad sister in her best clothes, and wound the donkey's tail round her head and fastened it down with hairpins and then covered her with a long veil.

Soon the Prince came back in a golden coach drawn by four splendid white horses. The widow and the wicked sister met him at the garden gate, where they curtsied low, and the Prince gallantly handed his bride into the coach.

"My love," said he, as soon as they were seated, "why do you keep this thick veil on?"

The wicked sister answered in a muffled voice, "Because I am crying so much at leaving my mother." So he let her keep the veil on.

On the way to the palace, however, they had to drive past the House of Cats, whereupon all the cats leaned out of the windows and called to the Prince, "Miaow, miaow! That is not your bride, that is her wicked sister! Miaow, miaow!"

Then the Prince pulled off the veil and saw how he had been deceived. He made the wicked sister get out of the carriage and he drove back at a gallop to the widow's cottage, where he demanded his bride. Muttering and complaining, the old woman let Lisina out of the cupboard, and Lisina threw herself into the Prince's arms.

They drove back to the palace in triumph and they were married that very day.

from Tuscany

2

Thirteenth

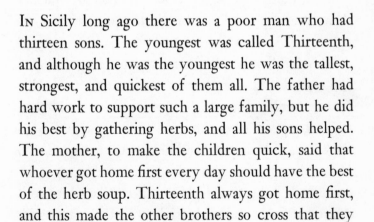

IN Sicily long ago there was a poor man who had thirteen sons. The youngest was called Thirteenth, and although he was the youngest he was the tallest, strongest, and quickest of them all. The father had hard work to support such a large family, but he did his best by gathering herbs, and all his sons helped. The mother, to make the children quick, said that whoever got home first every day should have the best of the herb soup. Thirteenth always got home first, and this made the other brothers so cross that they were always grumbling about it in the village.

Presently these grumbles reached the ears of the King of Sicily, and he said to his courtiers, "Perhaps this lad is quick enough to help us deal with the ogre. Bring Thirteenth to me."

This ogre lived with his ogress wife in a castle not far from the palace. He was very ugly, strong, and greedy, always robbing people and sometimes eating them, and everybody was afraid of him.

When Thirteenth appeared, the King said, "Now, you must go and steal the coverlet from the ogre's bed while he is asleep. That will be a lesson for him and I will give you a bag of gold."

"Your Majesty," cried Thirteenth, "how can I? If the ogre sees me, he will eat me."

"You must try," said the King. "You are quicker than everyone else. You should be quicker than the ogre."

Thirteenth went off reluctantly to the ogre's castle and waited behind the bushes outside until he saw the ogre go out hunting and the ogress go into the kitchen to cook supper. Then Thirteenth slipped quietly into the castle, stole upstairs, and hid under the ogre's bed. When the ogre came up to his bedroom that night, he said, "I smell the smell of a human! I will eat him up!" Thirteenth shivered with fright, but the ogress said, "Nonsense! No human has been near the castle all day!"

So they got into bed and were soon fast asleep.

When he heard the ogre snoring, Thirteenth gave a gentle pull at the coverlet to work it loose. The ogre wakened and roared out, "What's that?"

"Miaow! miaow!" said Thirteenth.

"It's only the cat," said the ogress. "Scat! Scat!" she called, clapping her hands.

Soon they were both snoring again.

Thirteenth crawled out, snatched the coverlet, and ran for his life. The ogre was after him in a flash. "I see you, Thirteenth! I'll catch you! I'll eat you!" he howled. But Thirteenth was too quick for him and soon reached the palace, while the ogre was left puffing and gasping far behind.

What rejoicing there was in the poor man's cottage when Thirteenth came home jingling a bag full of golden ducats! His brothers didn't grumble about him then. They all had a great feast and lived together happily, until the King sent for Thirteenth again.

"Now," said the King, "you must go and steal the ogre's horse. Then he will not be able to ride about the country robbing people as he does now. Bring me the horse and I will give you three bags of gold."

Thirteenth thought for a minute. "Your Majesty," he said, "if you will give me a bag of sweet cakes and a silk ladder with hooks at the end of it, I will see what I can do."

Late that night Thirteenth went to the ogre's castle. The gate was shut and barred, but he threw up the hooks until they caught on the top of the gate, and then he climbed the silk ladder and jumped down into the courtyard. Like a shadow, he crept to the stable. The horse whinnied and stamped, but when Thirteenth gave him a sweet cake, he was quiet again. Thirteenth gave him another cake and another and another and another until the horse was very friendly. Then Thirteenth climbed on its back and walked it quietly into the courtyard. But when he drew the bolts and swung open the gate, the hinges made a tremendous creaking, for they had not been oiled for a hundred years. The ogre wakened in a fury and came tumbling downstairs into the courtyard roaring, "Thirteenth! I see you! I'll eat you!"

Thirteenth was too quick for him. He clapped his heels to the horse's sides and galloped so fast that he had reached the palace before the ogre had puffed as far as the first milestone.

Thirteenth's family had three more bags of gold, and all lived together happily, until the King sent for him again.

"The ogre is still robbing and killing people," said the King. "He must be taken prisoner and brought to me, and you, Thirteenth, are the only man in Sicily quick enough and brave enough to do it."

"But, your Majesty, how can I? A dozen men could not hold him! He will kill me and eat me."

"You must find a way of doing it," answered the King, "and I will give you seven bags of gold."

There was no help for it. Thirteenth had to sit and think until he had thought of a plan. He got the King's carpenters to make a large strong chest with heavy iron hinges and bolts, and he loaded this on a little cart. He put on a gray beard and a gray wig, he dressed himself as a monk, and he trundled the little cart all the way to the ogre's castle.

"Mr. Ogre," he called, pulling at the bellrope. "Mr. Ogre!"

Very soon the ogre came to the gate to see what all the noise was about.

"Mr. Ogre," said the monk, speaking like an old man. "Does Thirteenth live here?"

"I wish he did," roared the ogre. "I'd break his neck. What do you want him for?"

"He has killed our abbot," said the monk. "I want to capture him and have him punished. But I don't know him. Do you?"

"Know him!" roared the ogre. "I do! I do!"

"How tall is he?" asked the monk.

"As tall as I am."

"When I've captured him," said the monk, "would this chest hold him?"

"I think so," answered the ogre.

"Well, if you're as tall as he is, will you get into the chest so that we can see?"

"I will," said the ogre. "Anything to help catch that rascal!" He climbed into the chest and lay down. "There, you can see it's a good fit."

"Let me try the lid," said Thirteenth, shutting it down and shooting the bolts. "Now, can you get out?"

The ogre struggled with all his might, but he could not break out.

"Splendid," said the lad in his own voice. "I am Thirteenth and I am taking you to the King."

The ogre howled and kicked and thumped his hardest, but it was no use. Thirteenth trundled the cart to the palace. The King threw the ogre into the palace dungeon, and put the ogress in with him, and they never killed or ate anyone again.

Then Thirteenth went home, jingling his seven bags full of ducats, and for the rest of their lives he and his family always had enough to eat.

from Sicily

3

The King Who Wanted
a Beautiful Wife

———◆———

ONCE upon a time the King of Sicily wanted to get married, but he was very hard to please. He looked at the pretty daughters of all the neighboring kings and princes, he looked at all the ladies of his own court, and not one of them seemed to him beautiful enough. So in the end he said to one of his servants, "You must go out in secret, without telling anyone what you are doing, and search my kingdom from end to end until you have found the most beautiful girl in the land. Bring her to me and I will marry her and reward you richly."

The young man set out on his quest. He visited

every town and village, every castle and cottage, and he found many beautiful girls, but not one who seemed to him *quite* beautiful enough to be the King's bride. At last, when he was in despair, he came to a little, tumble-down cottage in a dark wood. The door was shut and the window shuttered, but he could hear the whirr of a spinning wheel inside, so he knocked at the door.

The whirring stopped and a girlish voice said, "Who is there?"

"A traveler," answered the youth, "and I am very thirsty. Please, would you give me a drink of water?"

He felt sure this would make her open the door. But no! A little wicket in the shutter opened, and a delicate white hand held out a small pitcher of water.

This cottage was inhabited by two sisters. One of them was eighty years old, the other was ninety, and neither was beautiful. But, because they had spent all their lives spinning and weaving delicate thread and had never worked outdoors in the hot sun, their hands were still very beautiful. The young man thought the hand holding the pitcher was the most beautiful he had ever seen, and he felt sure that the owner of the hand must be altogether lovely. He hurried back to the King and told his story.

"Very well," said the King, "go back and try to see her."

Again the young man knocked at the cottage door, asking for water, and again the spinster handed the pitcher out to him through the little opening in the shutter.

"Fair maiden," he asked, "do you live here all alone?"

"No," she answered, "I live here with my sister. We are poor girls and we earn our living by spinning and weaving."

"How old are you?"

"I am fifteen," she said, because she was much too proud to admit the truth. "My sister is twenty."

When the King heard this, he said, "I will take the one who is fifteen. Go and bring her here."

For the third time the young man tapped at the cottage door, and when the wicket opened, he said, "Fair maiden, the King wants to make you his Queen. Will you marry him?"

"Gladly," she answered, "but never since my birth has a ray of sunshine fallen on me, and if I were to come out into the daylight I should go black all over. If you will ask the King to send a closed carriage for me at night, I will come to his palace."

That same night the King sent his gilded carriage, in which was a wonderful dress of cloth of gold, studded with precious stones. The spinster put it on, but she covered her face and head with a thick veil.

She looked very graceful as she walked into the great hall of the palace and curtsied low to the King, who came to greet her. He begged her to take off her veil.

"No," she said, "I dare not. The candles and torches are far too bright."

The King was so enchanted by her beautiful voice and beautiful hands that he married her then and there, without seeing her face, and led her in triumph into his chamber. But when he took off her veil and saw how he had been deceived, he lost his temper and threw the old woman out of the window.

She might well have been dashed to pieces in the courtyard far below, but her clothes caught on a big nail that was sticking out of the wall, and there she hung between heaven and earth.

As the palace clock was striking midnight, four fairies came floating by.

"Look," said one of them, "there is the old woman who cheated our godson the King. Shall we wish her dress to tear and let her fall?"

"Oh, no!" cried the youngest fairy. "Let us wish

her well, for the King's sake. I wish her to be young again."

"And I wish her to be the most beautiful girl in the land," cried the second.

"And I wish her a good heart," cried the third.

"And I will give her wisdom."

At that the old woman was transformed. But she still hung there, and she was very frightened, and very sorry now for the trick she had played.

When the King awoke next morning, he was horrified to think that he had thrown the old woman out of the window. He ran to look out and he could hardly believe his eyes when he saw a lovely young girl hanging from her veil.

Reaching out, he pulled her into the room, and they fell into each other's arms. Then they had a splendid feast to celebrate their wedding, and everyone agreed that the Queen was the most lovely lady in the land. So they lived together happily because of the good gifts which the fairies had given her.

One day the Queen's old sister grew tired of living alone, spinning and weaving in the dark cottage in the wood, and came to the Palace, asking to see the Queen.

"Who is this queer creature?" said the King.

"Oh, she is a relative of mine," said the Queen. "She is very old. Let us be kind to her."

The King and Queen entertained her royally, and she did not dare to give away the Queen's secret, but when they were alone together she pestered and nagged at the Queen to tell her how to get herself changed, too.

Finally the Queen said, "It was quite easy. I had my old skin taken off and this new one was underneath." Off went the old woman to the village barber, who was also the surgeon, and asked him to take off her skin.

"I can't!" he cried. "You would die if I did."

But she wouldn't take no for an answer. She pestered and nagged at him until at last he sat her down in his chair and took out his sharpest knife. Then he made a little cut on her forehead, and it hurt so much that she leaped out of the chair and ran screaming out of the shop. She never left her cottage again, but the Queen sent her many presents to make her happy.

from Sicily

4

The Animal Princes

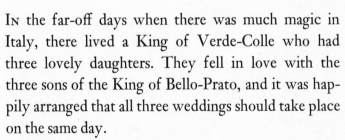

In the far-off days when there was much magic in Italy, there lived a King of Verde-Colle who had three lovely daughters. They fell in love with the three sons of the King of Bello-Prato, and it was happily arranged that all three weddings should take place on the same day.

Then a very sad thing happened. The King of Bello-Prato offended a fairy by not asking her to the banquet that he gave to mark the three engagements. She took her revenge by enchanting the three Princes. She turned one into a falcon, one into a stag, and the third into a dolphin. The King of Verde-Colle would not let his daughters marry these creatures, and the Princesses were heartbroken.

But the three Princes were not to be beaten. The falcon called together all the birds of the air. Chaffinches, wrens, bullfinches, cuckoos, magpies, skylarks, and the rest came by the thousand. The falcon told his story and asked them to strip the gardens of Verde-Colle of all their leaves and flowers. They did this with a will, so that there was not a leaf or flower left on any bush or tree.

The stag called on the animals of Italy. Rams, goats, hares, rabbits, and porcupines, beyond number, came to do his bidding, and he sent them to Verde-Colle. There they left not a growing seed, not a young plant, not a single blade of grass.

Last, the dolphin, with a hundred sea monsters, raised such a fearful storm along the coast of Verde-Colle that every ship and boat was dashed to pieces.

Now the King could only give way, before his kingdom was completely ruined. Very sadly he sent his three beautiful daughters to Bello-Prato, but before they went the Queen their mother had three gold rings made, all exactly alike, and gave one to each princess. "Whatever happens," she said, "you will always know one another by these rings."

As soon as they were all married, the falcon carried

off his bride, the Princess Fabiella, to a palace on the top of a high mountain, and the stag took Vasta, the second sister, to a mansion with wonderful gardens, in the heart of a forest. The dolphin took Rita, the youngest, on his back and swam with her far across the sea to a palace built on an island. So the three Princesses lived like queens.

Not long after they had gone, a son was born to the King and Queen of Verde-Colle, whom they named Titone, and in the course of time he grew into a fine young man. One day his mother told him about his sisters and he made up his mind to go out into the world to find them, although no one knew where they were or what had happened to them.

At last the King agreed to let him go, and the Queen gave him a ring just like those she had given the Princesses. For weeks he traveled on, from one end of Italy to the other. At last he came to the foot of the mountain, where an old man told him that the Princess Fabiella lived in the palace at the top. When he reached it, he stood gazing in wonder, for it was built of gold and silver and the finest marble, and Fabiella, looking out of a window, saw him and sent a servant to bring him to her.

"Who are you?" she asked. "And where do you come from?"

Bowing low to this beautiful lady, he said, "I am Titone, Prince of Verde-Colle. Are you not my sister Fabiella?" He showed her his ring, and when she compared it with her own, she was sure he was her brother. They embraced, for they were very happy to meet.

Fabiella was afraid that her husband, the falcon, might be angry, so she hid Titone in a cupboard, and when the falcon came home from hunting, she said, "Dear husband, I long to see my father and mother again. Could we not visit them?"

"That must wait," he replied, "until I feel like carrying you there."

"Then," she said, "could we not send for some of my relatives to come and see me?"

"Who would come to see you in this distant place?" he asked.

"Well, if any did come, would you be angry?"

"No, indeed," answered the falcon. "I should be very glad to see them for your sake."

At this Fabiella brought Titone from the cupboard, and the falcon made him very welcome. Titone stayed for a fortnight and then he said he must go on to look for his other sisters, so they all said goodbye, very sadly. Fabiella sent many messages to her father and mother.

Then the falcon pulled a feather from his breast and gave it to Titone, saying, "Keep this carefully, and if you are ever in great need or danger, throw this feather on the ground and say, 'Come, come!' and I will come to you."

Titone thanked him, put the feather in his purse, and went on his way.

For months he wandered here and there, through wilds and wolds, until good luck brought him to the mansion in the forest where Vasta lived with the stag. She saw him and called him in, and as soon as he saw the ring on her finger, he showed his own and they fell into each other's arms. The stag was very kind to him, so they were all happy together, but after a fortnight Titone felt that he must go on his way again. At parting, the stag pulled a hair from his breast, saying, "Keep this, Titone, and if ever you need me, throw it on the ground and say, 'Come, come!'"

Now the most difficult part of his quest had come, for he knew the dolphin lived in the sea. He took ship and sailed here and there, visiting many lands and islands, until at long last he found Rita on the dolphin's island. They were both very glad to see him

29

and he lived happily with them, but in the end he said he must go home to give his father and mother the news of his three sisters. Sadly they said goodbye, and the dolphin gave him a piece from one of its flippers, saying, "If you should ever need me, throw this on the ground and cry, 'Come, come!' And I will appear."

When the ship landed him in Italy, Titone bought a horse and set out at once for Verde-Colle, meeting with no adventures until he came into a dark forest. There he found a lake with an island in it, and on the island a grim tower. At one of the windows he saw a beautiful maiden sitting beside a hideous dragon which was fast asleep. As soon as she saw Titone, she called to him softly, "Save me, save me from this dragon! It keeps me prisoner here and I am dying of misery."

"That I would do gladly," he answered, "but how can I cross the lake, and climb the tower, and do battle with such a monster?"

Then he remembered. Opening his purse, he threw the feather, the hair, and the piece of the dolphin's flipper on the ground, and cried, "Come, come!"

Instantly the earth opened and the falcon, the stag, and the dolphin appeared. "Here we are," they cried. "What are your wishes?"

"All I wish," said Titone, "is that this beautiful maiden be saved from the claws of the dragon, and the evil tower turned into a heap of ruins."

The falcon called up two griffins, fierce creatures with lions' bodies and eagles' wings and claws. They flew silently to the tower, lifted the maiden through the window, and put her down gently at the lakeside, where Titone and the three animal Princes were standing. Titone thought her even more beautiful now that she was so close. He comforted her, for she was very frightened, but at that moment the dragon opened its flaming eyes, sprang into the lake, and began to swim straight toward them, breathing out fire and smoke as it came. Certainly it would have killed them all, had not the stag called a company of lions and tigers to their aid. Roaring terribly, they flung themselves on the dragon and tore it to pieces. Then they and the griffins disappeared as suddenly as they had come.

"Now it is my turn," said the dolphin. He commanded the waters of the lake to rise and they battered down the tower and swept over the island so that nothing was left of them.

"Thank you, thank you," said the maiden. "I cannot thank you enough, but I am the daughter of the

King of Chiara. If you will come with me to him, he will reward you all."

"We have our reward already," answered the falcon. "The fairy who enchanted us said that we should never return to human shape unless we rescued a king's daughter from great danger. Ever since then, we have longed for this moment."

As he spoke, he and the other two turned into handsome men. They were the Princes of Bello-Prato once again!

When they had all embraced Titone, the three of them cried out together, "Come, come, come!"

In a few minutes, a splendid carriage appeared, drawn by six lions, and in the carriage were the three Princesses, Fabiella, Vasta, and Rita. What joy it was to them to see their husbands human once again! How gladly they welcomed Titone and the Princess of Chiara! How much they had to tell each other!

Soon the carriage was carrying them all swiftly to Verde-Colle, where they were received with rejoicing such as the kingdom had never known, and before it was over, the Prince Titone married the beautiful Princess of Chiara.

from Naples

5

A Little Bird

An old countryman and his wife used to earn their living by working hard all day in the fields, and they got more and more tired of it.

One hot day, when they were having a rest in the shade of a wall, the woman said to her husband, "We are so poor, and we have to work so hard, and it's all the fault of Adam and Eve. If they hadn't been so silly as to pick the fruit from the only tree in the Garden of Eden which they were forbidden to touch, we should still be in Paradise. We should be living in a beautiful garden, with nothing to do except enjoy ourselves."

"Yes," said her husband. "How silly they were! I wish we'd been there instead of Adam and Eve. Why, the whole human race would still be in Paradise, as you say."

It happened that the Duke was riding by on the other side of the wall, and he heard what they said, so he called to them to come and speak to him. They were rather scared, but they came. The old man took off his hat and bowed; the old woman curtsied. The Duke smiled at them both.

"I couldn't help hearing what you said about Adam and Eve," he told them, "and I think it's only fair for you to have the same chance that they had. How would you like it if I took you into my palace to live, and gave you the finest food and wine, and servants to wait on you, and every luxury?"

"Oh, that would be wonderful," cried the old man. "That would be paradise for us. Oh, thank you, my lord, thank you!" And they bowed and curtsied again.

"Good," said the Duke. "There is only one condition. In Paradise there was one tree that Adam and Eve were forbidden to touch. On my table there will always be one dish with a cover on it, and you must never lift the cover. Can you promise that?"

"Oh, yes, my lord," they said in chorus. "Indeed, we can promise that."

"Then follow me to my palace," replied the Duke, "and I will do everything I can to make you happy."

They were in fact very happy. They had rooms to themselves. They were given fine clothes to wear, and soft beds to sleep in, and the best food and drink that the Duke's kitchen could provide. Meanwhile, the Duke sent for one of his servants and said, "I want you to catch a bullfinch without hurting it and put it into a large dish with a silver cover. Put the dish in the middle of the table every time the old man and his wife are having a meal, and wait on them yourself, so that you can tell me if they ever lift the cover. They have promised not to."

The servant did as he was told, and he said to the old couple, "This is the forbidden dish."

"Yes," they replied. "We have promised never to lift the cover. And why should we want to?"

The days went by and the weeks went by, and at first they were quite happy in the palace. But they had nothing to do except eat, and they got more and more greedy and peevish. At first they were delighted with two good dishes for a meal, for the food was far better than any they had ever tasted before; they had lived on beans at home. But presently they asked for three dishes, then four, then five, until they had an enormous dinner of seven or eight courses, and weren't contented even with that.

"Don't you get tired of having the same food every day?" said the wife.

"Yes," answered her husband, "soups and omelettes, and spaghetti, fish and crabs, and crayfish and lobsters and oysters and prawns, beef and mutton and pork and venison, quails and chicken and ducks and swans and peacocks and turkeys, and only fourteen different sweetmeats, or perhaps fifteen—they just go round and round, don't they? Really, it's time we had something new, isn't it?"

"Yes," agreed his wife, and she called to the servant, "Here, you, bring us something new."

"I am sorry, madam," replied the servant, "but you always have the same food as the Duke himself. There is nothing new we can give you."

"There is this dish which is never uncovered," said the wife.

"We mustn't touch that," said the husband quickly. "Although . . . well, it must have something rare in it, for it has a silver cover. None of the dishes we are served ever has a silver cover. It isn't fair."

"We mustn't think about it," said the wife. "But

. . . perhaps if we just lifted the cover a very little and just peeped underneath, it wouldn't do any harm."

They looked at the dish for a few minutes. "Well, lifting one corner wouldn't be opening it, would it?" the husband said.

"We'd better leave it alone and stop thinking about it," said the wife.

They sat and looked at the dish, until presently the wife said, "If we just peeped, it couldn't do any harm, could it? What *can* the Duke have put in it?"

"I can't even begin to guess," replied the husband, "and I can't see what difference it would make to him if we did look."

"No, that's what I think," she said. "It wouldn't hurt him, would it?"

"I don't see how it could," said the husband.

Very carefully the wife lifted one corner of the cover just a little. Neither of them could see anything. She lifted the cover a little more.

Out flew the bullfinch and fluttered through the window.

Off went the servant to tell the Duke.

When he came in, the two were still staring help-lessly at the empty dish.

"Well," said he, "you've broken your promise, but

I shall keep mine. Away you go, back to your cottage. You may be happier there than you've been here. And don't find fault with Adam and Eve again."

They didn't.

from Rome

6

The Simple Youth

———◆———

THERE was a merchant once who was as rich as the
sea, but he had one great sorrow: his only son was so
simple and ignorant that he hardly knew a fritter from
a cucumber. At last the man could bear the lad's folly
no longer. He put a purse stuffed with gold ducats
into his hand and said, "Take this, and go out into the
world. Go to the East, go to Cairo, and see if you can
learn some sense."

Moscione, for that was the lad's name, mounted his
horse and set off toward Venice, the grand marketplace of the world, intending to take ship there for
Cairo.

At the end of his first day's journey he saw a youth

standing against a poplar tree, and said to him, "O youth, who are you? Where do you come from, and what is your trade?"

The youth answered, "My name is Furgolo, I come from Saetta, and I can run as fast as lightning."

"I should like to see you run," said Moscione.

At that moment a deer went bounding by, going like the wind. Furgolo gave it a long start, then he set off, and in four strides he had come up with it. Moscione, marveling, said, "Will you come with me? I will pay you a good wage."

Furgolo agreed, so they went on together, Furgolo walking at the stirrup, and soon they came upon another youth. "My name is Hare's Ear," he told them. "I come from Valle-Curiosa, and when I put my ear to the ground, I can hear anything that is happening anywhere in the world, even the curses of sailors at sea."

"If this is true," said Moscione, "tell me what my father and mother are talking about at home."

Hare's Ear put his ear to the ground, and a few moments later he said, "An old man is saying to his wife, 'What a good thing it is that that simpleton Moscione has gone out into the world. He may come back a man!'"

"It is enough," cried Moscione. "You speak the truth. Come with me, and I will give you a good wage."

So the three went on together, and they had hardly gone ten miles when they met a third youth, who was carrying a crossbow, "Who are you, and what can you do in this world?" asked Moscione.

"My name is Hit Straight," he answered. "I come from Castiello, and when I shoot with my crossbow I can hit an apple in the center." There was a bean on the top of a stone a bowshot away. Hit Straight fitted an arrow to his bow, pulled the string, and hit the bean without touching the stone.

"There is no doubt about it," said Moscione, "you too must enter my service."

That night they stayed at an inn and next day went on their way toward Venice, until they came to a little seaport where men were building a pier in the scorching heat of the sun. Moscione reined in his horse to watch them. "My masters," said he, "how is it you can work so hard in this terrible heat? Not even an ox could work as you are doing."

One of them answered, "We are as cool and fresh as a rose, because this youth behind us blows at us as though all the west winds were blowing."

"Let me see him," said Moscione, and when the youth came he asked, "What is your name, where do you come from, what is your trade?"

"My name is Sciosci, I come from Terra-Ventosa, and I can imitate all the winds of heaven by blowing with my mouth." He blew at three plum trees that were standing half a mile away, and uprooted them all.

So he too joined their company, and the five of them journeyed on. Very soon they met another youth, who told them, "My name is Forte, I come from Valentino, and I can carry a mountain on my back as though it were a feather. Try me, fair sir!"

They heaped on his back every stone that they could carry from the hillside, and a score of giant tree trunks that the woodmen had felled, until the five of them could carry no more. Forte laughed and walked off with the load as though he were carrying nothing at all.

"You must come and join us!" cried Moscione and Forte gladly agreed.

That evening Moscione and his followers came to the fair city of Bello-Sciore, and went to an inn. While they sat at dinner they asked the innkeeper for the news of that place, and he told them that the King had a daughter named Clantella who could run like the wind and was so light of foot that she could run across a field of flowers without breaking one of them. The Princess had declared that she would marry only a man who could outpace her, and the King had proclaimed it far and wide that the Princess would give her hand to any man who could win two races with her.

As soon as they had finished dinner, Moscione went to the palace, and it was arranged that he should try his fortune next morning. When the time came, he sent a message to the King, saying that he was ill and asking that one of his followers might run in his place. The Princess agreed, and Furgolo went his way to the great square. Every terrace and balcony and window was packed with people gathered to watch the race. Furgolo took his stand at the starting point, where Clantella joined him, wearing a short skirt and small thin shoes, pretty and tight-fitting.

A trumpet sounded, and off they went like hares when greyhounds are at their heels. Swift as the Princess was, Furgolo reached the mark before her, and the whole crowd roared and stamped like mad, shouting, "Well done the foreigner, well done the foreigner!" But the Princess went away scarlet with shame and speechless with anger.

The second race was to be run next morning, and she swore she would not be beaten again by such a varlet as Furgolo. As soon as she got back to the palace, she enchanted a ring so that anyone who tried to run while wearing it would find his feet like lead and his knees giving way under him. Then she sent this to Furgolo, asking him to wear it for her sake.

Next morning Furgolo set out for the great square, wearing the ring, but Hare's Ear put his ear to the ground and heard the Princess telling the King what she had done. Hare's Ear told his friends and Hit Straight took his bow to the square.

When the race started, Clantella was off like the wind, leaving Furgolo stumbling along behind her. Then Hit Straight, drawing his bow to the hilt, let fly an arrow that split the magic ring on Furgolo's finger, just where the charm lay hidden. Instantly Furgolo recovered and in three strides he had passed the Princess and reached the winning post ahead of her. Once again the crowd cheered madly and Clantella, blushing scarlet, went away without a word.

The King asked himself anxiously what he should do. He did not want to give his daughter to this young foreigner, who might be a penniless knave, and the Princess declared she would never marry him. The King called his wise men, and they said he should offer Moscione a rich reward instead of the Princess's hand in marriage.

The King and the Princess were delighted with this, so a messenger was sent to Moscione. He replied that he would accept the offer if the King would give him as much silver and gold as one of his followers could carry. "Agreed!" cried the King, overjoyed that Moscione had asked so little.

Forte went at once to the King's treasury. There they loaded bars of gold and sacks of silver on his broad back, one after another, until the Treasury was completely empty, and Forte carried it all as though it were nothing. They brought all the money from all the banks, and from all the money-changers and moneylenders in the city. The King stripped his palace of all his golden goblets, plates, and dishes, but Forte still stood like a tower. The King sent to all his knights and barons, and their servants came staggering under the weight of golden dishes and silver candlesticks, chains and rings, and all the coins their masters possessed. Still Forte asked for more, until there was nothing left to give him. Then at last he set off along the road, with Moscione and the others beside him.

When the King's wise men saw all the wealth of the kingdom disappearing like this, they said to him, "Sire, this is a great folly. Will you not send your army to lighten that man's load?"

"Indeed I will!" cried the King, and dispatched a company of his horse guards to bring back the treasure. But Hare's Ear had been listening to what they said, and he told his companions. As soon as the guards came in sight, Sciosci blew such a tempest at them that they were swept backward down the road and out of sight.

Then the young men went happily on their way to Moscione's home, where he divided his riches fairly among his followers and gave a large share to his father, who never complained again that his son was a simpleton.

from Naples

7

A Crumb in His Beard

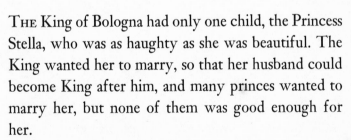

The King of Bologna had only one child, the Princess Stella, who was as haughty as she was beautiful. The King wanted her to marry, so that her husband could become King after him, and many princes wanted to marry her, but none of them was good enough for her.

The poor King was more and more worried by this, for he was getting old. At last he made a plan. He asked all the unmarried kings and princes in Italy to a feast in the palace, and the Princess was to hide behind a screen in the hall so that she could look at them all carefully, without their knowing, and make up her mind which of them might please her.

You can imagine what a splendid feast it was. All the plates were of gold and silver. The food and wines were the very finest that could be found in the whole of Italy. In every corner of the hall a fountain threw sweet perfumes into the air, a thousand candles burned in the great chandeliers, and hidden musicians played soft music. As the kings and princes, in their richest clothes, sat down at the long table, the Princess and one of her ladies hid themselves behind a screen with a peephole on it through which they could see everything that was going on.

"Look, Your Highness," said the lady, "that young Prince in green silk sitting next to the Queen—don't you think he's handsome?"

"No," said the Princess, "his nose is too big."

"And the one on your father's right hand?"

"His eyes are like saucers," said the Princess.

"And the one beside him?"

"The one in pink?" asked the Princess. "How could I possibly marry a man who wears pink?"

So it went on, all round the table. The Princess found fault with their mouths or their manners or the color of their hair, until they came to the last, a very handsome young Prince with a fine beard, who sat near the screen. Even the Princess could find nothing wrong with him, until suddenly she cried in disgust:

"Oh, he has a crumb in his beard. What a dirty man he must be!"

Now the young Prince was sitting so near the screen that he heard these words. He guessed it was the Princess speaking, and he was so angry that he made up his mind to punish her. As soon as the banquet was over, he spoke to the King, who liked him very much, and together they made a plan, which they agreed to keep secret. Then the King sent for the Princess and asked her which of the guests pleased her most.

"None of them," she said, "except perhaps the young Prince of Green Hill, but he had a crumb in his beard, and I couldn't possibly marry a man who is as dirty as that."

"Take warning, my daughter," answered the King. "One day your pride will make you suffer." Then he said no more.

The palace was built in the middle of the city, and one window of the Princess Stella's bedchamber looked out on a quiet street in which there was a baker's shop.

A few nights after the feast, when all the kings and princes had gone home in disgust, Stella was just going to bed when she heard a man's voice from the street singing a love song so sweetly that it went to her heart. She ran to the window and listened spellbound until the song was done. Then she said to her maid: "Who was that singing so wonderfully? I must know. Find out who he is."

Next day the maid told her that the singer was the young man who sifted the flour in the bakery, and that evening the princess listened as before. Next morning she got up very early and watched for the singer to come out. He was a young man, clean-shaven and graceful, and dressed in shabby clothes. She thought him the most handsome man she had ever seen. When he looked up and saw her, he took off his cap and bowed to her, and she smiled her sweetest smile.

Stella was enchanted. She watched every morning, and from bowing and smiling they soon got to talking together, for the window was not very high. He told her his name was Pippo. That evening he sang a love song under her window, playing a guitar. Next morning they spoke of love, and in a few days Pippo said, "My sweet lady, will you marry me?"

"There is nothing else in the world that I want," she answered, and threw him a kiss. "But what have you got to live on?"

"I haven't a penny," said Pippo.

"It does not matter," she said. "I have enough money for us both." That day she put together her jewels and all the money she could get, tying them into a bundle. That evening she lowered the bundle on a rope to the young man and asked him to sell all the things so that they would have money enough to live in royal style.

Two nights later she climbed down the rope, and hand in hand they fled from the city. After walking half the night, they reached a large town where they soon found a priest. He married them at once. Then Pippo led Stella away to a poor house in a shabby side street, and down a long passage to a little room at the back. "This is our home," he said.

Stella was horrified. The room was dirty, there was only one window, high above their heads, and the only furniture was a straw mattress on the floor, a wooden bench, and an old table. "What's the matter?" said her husband. "Don't you like the place? Don't you know I am a poor man?"

"But what have you done with the things I gave you?"

"I owed a lot of money," he answered, "and I used them to pay my debts."

There was nothing she could do. There they spent

the night, and in the morning Pippo brought out a ragged dress and clumsy boots and said, "You must wear these and go to work."

Stella burst into tears, but he said, "That won't help you. Do as I tell you, or I shall beat you until you do. I am a porter in the King's palace in this city, and today is their washing day. You must come and help with the washing."

Very sadly Stella followed him and she spent a miserable day in the laundry, working hard for the first time in her life, and came home tired out. All her pride was gone now. She cried and cried, and begged Pippo not to send her to work next day, but he said it was baking day and she must go and work in the kitchen. The following day there was to be a great feast, followed by a ball, and although Stella cried more than ever, Pippo made her spend the day in getting food ready and washing dishes.

When the feasting was over, the dancing began, and as the poor girl heard the music in the distance, she thought sadly of her old life as a princess. At that moment Pippo appeared in the kitchen. Taking her by the arm, he dragged her, dressed in rags as she was, into the ballroom, where he presented her to the King and Queen of that city as his wife. Stella was so ashamed that she fainted.

When she recovered, she was lying on a sofa, with the Queen bending over her and the King and Pippo watching anxiously.

"Stella," said the Queen, "your trials are over. Pippo is our son, the Crown Prince. He has treated you like this only to cure your pride, but he has done more than enough. Now you shall be a princess again."

Then Pippo begged her to forgive him and she was so happy she did it gladly. The Queen led her to another room, where her own most beautiful dress was put on her by her own maid. Then her father the King of Bologna came in and embraced her tenderly, for he too had been in on the plot.

Last of all, Pippo himself appeared, dressed like a prince once again, but as he pointed out, he had no crumbs in his beard. In fact, he had no beard. He had shaved it off to disguise himself. Proudly he led his beautiful wife to the ballroom, and after that happy evening they had a happy life.

from Bologna

8

The Wonderful Stone

NARDIELLO was a poor old man who lived in the city of Grotta-Negra. He was so old that he could work no longer and so poor that he had nothing left but a brass finger ring and a little cock. He had sold everything else to buy bread and beans, and at last he made up his mind that he must sell the cock too.

On his way to the market, he was stopped by two strange men who were magicians in disguise and who offered him half a ducat for the cock. They said they would pay him at once if he would carry it to their house, so he followed them along the road, well pleased with his bargain. Presently they began to talk in whispers and he managed to overhear them.

"Jennarone," said one, "this cock will make our fortunes . . . How lucky we are! When we have taken the magic stone from its head and set it in a ring, we can get anything we wish for."

"Hold your tongue, Jacovo," answered the other angrily. "I see myself rich already, but it is very unlucky to talk about it."

Now Nardiello had traveled in many countries and eaten bread from many bakers' shops. He knew his way about. He took to his heels, and as soon as he reached his little hut, he killed the cock and took the stone from its head. He set the stone at once in the brass ring that he wore, and then he said, "I wish I were a handsome youth, eighteen years old."

Hardly had he spoken the words than he was transformed. "I wish for a mirror in a golden frame," he said. At once it was put into his hand, and he looked at himself in joy and amazement. He was young, tall, and strong, and as good-looking as a beautiful day in spring.

"I wish for wonderful clothes and a wonderful palace," he cried. "I wish to be a cousin of the King's!"

Instantly a sumptuous palace rose from the earth, with rooms marvelous to see and furnishings that had no equal in Italy. There were the most wonderful paintings on the walls, and the coffers were full of gold and precious stones. Servants in rich liveries of blue and silver stood awaiting his commands, there was a great gilded coach in the courtyard, and the stables were full of noble horses.

Nardiello lost no time in giving a grand banquet for the King, who was so impressed by all he saw that when Nardiello asked for the hand of the beautiful Princess Natalia, he readily agreed. The Princess was happy too, for Nardiello was as charming as he was rich, and in a few days the wedding was celebrated with the greatest festivities the kingdom had ever seen.

In the meantime the two magicians were plotting to get the ring. They made a very beautiful doll, which by magic danced and sang. Then they disguised themselves as merchants and when Nardiello was away hunting they went to his palace. Natalia was fascinated by the doll.

"What is the price?" she asked.

"No money can buy it," answered Jennarone, "but we will give it to you if you will grant our request. Your husband always wears a very curious ring on his left hand, and I have long wanted one like it, but he won't lend it to me. If you could let me have it, just long enough for me to get a copy made, I would gladly give you this doll."

The Princess was so bewitched by the doll that she said, "Come back in the morning and I will lend you the ring." That evening she coaxed her husband into letting her wear the ring for a little while, and next day she handed it over to the two magicians in exchange for the doll. Instantly they vanished to a forest near the city, leaving the Princess Natalia in great fear.

In the forest Jennarone, with the ring on his finger, said, "I wish that Nardiello should be just as he used to be."

At that moment Nardiello, in his richest clothes, was sitting talking with the King. Suddenly the King found himself talking to an old beggar with white hair, dressed in dirty rags. He was aghast. He called for his servants to drive the man out. Nardiello went to look for his palace, and found nothing except the miserable hut in which he used to live. The Princess was sitting beside it, weeping bitterly.

"Give me back my ring," he cried. "I am Nardiello, and I have been bewitched."

Sobbing, she told him the whole story, and he set out at once to look for the two magicians.

He traveled for days without getting any news of them, until at last he reached the Kingdom of the Mice. They thought he was a spy from the Kingdom of the Cats, so they dragged him before their king, but when he had told his story they were all sorry for him. The Mouse King called his council together to decide what could be done to help Nardiello.

Two of the oldest of the mice, Rudolo and Salta-riello, spoke up at once. They were wise in the ways of the world because they had lived for years in the Horn Tavern, which stood by the highroad, and many great folk stayed there.

"Three days ago," said Rudolo, "we were in the tavern when two men from Castle Rampino, who were passing that way, came in to eat. When they had finished their food and seen the bottoms of their tank-ards, they began to talk about the fine trick they had played on an old man in Grotta-Negra, whose ring they had taken from him."

As you can imagine, Nardiello was very much cheered by this. "If you will guide me to Castle Rampino," he said, "and help me to get back my ring, I will give you a whole cheese and a leg of salt pork."

The two mice agreed, and got leave from their king to go. All three set off that very day for the castle, which they reached in a few days. Then Nar-diello rested under the trees by the river while the two mice crept into the castle. They soon found that Jennarone never took the ring from his finger, so they had to wait for night. As soon as Jennarone was sound asleep, Rudolo crept into his bed and began to gnaw at his ring finger until he pulled off the ring and put it on a table beside the bed. Saltariello climbed on the table and picked up the ring in his teeth. Then the two mice took it to Nardiello.

When he saw the ring again, he was as happy as a man who is reprieved when he is just going to be hanged.

Thanking the two wise mice a thousand times, Nardiello slipped the ring on his finger and cried, "I wish myself young and rich as I was before!" Instantly his back straightened, his hair darkened, his eyes shone, his dirty rags turned into silks and velvets, and he was a handsome youth once more.

"I wish those magicians to be turned into donkeys and to come here at my command!" In a few moments the two donkeys came trotting through the trees. He wished onto one of them two large panniers filled with cheese and pork and lard, and set the two mice on the donkey's back. He wished a handsome saddle onto the other and climbed gaily on it himself. When they reached the Kingdom of the Mice, he gave the laden donkey to the Mouse King.

"Sire," he said, bowing low, "I thank you and your people with all my heart for all that you have done for me, and I pray heaven that neither trap nor snare nor poison shall ever do you harm, nor any cat annoy you."

Taking leave of them, he rode on to Grotta-Negra, where he found his palace restored to all its splendor, and his wife, the beautiful Princess Natalia, waiting for him. She wept again, but this time it was for joy. The King her father gave him a warm welcome too, and the donkey he chased away into the forest. You may be sure that Nardiello never let the magic stone leave his finger again.

from Naples

9

The Donkey Which Made Gold

IN A village in Tuscany there lived a poor widow with her little boy, who was not at all clever but was all she had. She tried to make a living by weaving, but times were hard and no matter how long she worked at her loom the two of them never had enough to eat and their clothes were in rags.

At last the poor woman felt she must ask for help, and the only person she could ask was her brother-in-law, who was a rich man's steward and lived in a town at some distance. One day she said to her little boy, "My son, you must go to your uncle and tell him how poor we are. I am sure he will help us."

The boy set off very early next morning. The road

was long and dusty, the sun was fierce, and he got so hot and tired that when he came to an inn he longed to get something to eat and drink. But he had no money, and there was nothing to do but go on.

At last he reached his uncle's fine house and told his story. That good man said, "I am very sorry to hear this. I wish you had come to me sooner. I will give you something to make sure that you are never short of money again. I will give you this little gray donkey. When you want money, all you have to do is hang this nosebag over its head and say, 'Donkey, donkey, give me gold.' Then it will fill the nosebag to the top with shining golden ducats. But, remember, you must not tell anyone except your mother about this, and you must not be parted from the donkey for a moment before you get home."

The boy thanked him and set out happily for home, riding the little donkey. By the time he reached the inn he was so tired that he could go no farther, and he said to himself, "Well, I can have all the money I want now, so why shouldn't I stay here and enjoy myself?"

He tethered his donkey beside the inn door, called for macaroni and white wine, and ate his supper while he watched the donkey cropping the road-side grass. Then he called the innkeeper and said he wanted a bedroom for the night, for the donkey and himself.

"The donkey can go in the stable," said the inn-keeper, "and you can have the best bedroom, at the foot of the stairs."

"No, no," said the boy, "I cannot be parted from my donkey."

Well, they argued it to and fro, but in the end the innkeeper gave way and the boy led the donkey into the bedroom. As soon as he had shut the door he hung the nosebag over the donkey's head and said, "Donkey, donkey, give me gold!" Then he counted out the gold ducats—there were twenty-one of them —and put them carefully in his pocket. Then he lay down on the bed and in next to no time he was fast asleep.

The innkeeper thought it very queer for anyone to want a donkey in his bedroom—he had never heard of such a thing—so as soon as the bedroom door was shut, he looked through a crack in the door and saw everything that happened.

"I must have that donkey," he said to himself. He waited until the boy was fast asleep, then he crept into the room and very quietly led the donkey away to the stable. There he had a little gray donkey of his own, very like the boy's, so he led it into the bedroom. The boy did not stir.

Next morning the boy was up betimes. He had his breakfast, paid his bill with a gold ducat, and rode away happily enough. The innkeeper went round to the stable, made three bagfuls of gold, and then hid the magic donkey away in a little room at the back of the inn.

When the boy had ridden a few miles down the road, he noticed a black mark on the donkey's neck which he had not seen before. Then he saw that the donkey's ears were a different color.

He climbed down and hung the donkey's nosebag over its head and asked it to make gold, but it only tried to eat the nosebag. So he rode back to the inn and asked the innkeeper for his own donkey. The innkeeper was very angry. "What do you mean?" he cried. "Do you think we have thieves in this house? Be off with you!" And he reached for his cudgel.

There was nothing the boy could do but ride back to his uncle and tell him the whole story.

"Well," said the steward, "it was not your fault, so I will give you this magic tablecloth. When you spread it out and ask it to give you a meal, it will serve all the food you can want, the most delicious food in the world. But, remember, you must not be parted from it and you must not tell anyone about it before you get home."

The boy thanked him gratefully and set off for home again, but by the time he reached the inn he was too tired to go any farther. This time he put his donkey in the stable and went to his bedroom without having supper. This made the rascally innkeeper very curious, so once again he peeped through the crack in the door. As the boy was hungry, he spread out the tablecloth on the table and said, "O tablecloth, give me food."

At once it was covered with meats and sweetmeats, apples and oranges and flasks of wine, and such an appetizing smell came through the door that it made the innkeeper's mouth water. "I must have that tablecloth," he said to himself, and went to get one of his own which looked very much like it.

When the boy had finished his supper, it was cleared by invisible hands. He left the cloth on the table and was soon fast asleep. Then the innkeeper crept in and exchanged the cloths.

Next morning the boy set off early. As soon as he was out of sight of the inn, he sat down by the wayside and asked the tablecloth to produce a good breakfast for him and a bundle of hay for the donkey. No food appeared. He tried again, and again nothing happened. Then he saw that the innkeeper had robbed him once more. He climbed on the donkey and rode back to his uncle as fast as he could.

This time the steward was angry. "You silly boy!" he cried. "Have you so little sense that you let that scoundrel rob you twice? You don't deserve any more help."

The little boy burst into tears. "No, sir," he sobbed. "I know I don't. I am so sorry, sir. But my mother, sir! My poor mother!"

"Yes, indeed," answered the steward, calming down a little. "Your poor mother ought to be helped. And that innkeeper ought to be punished. So I will give you this stick." He gave the boy a handsome walking cane, straight and strong, with a heavy golden knob. "This is a magic stick. If you say to it, 'Beat him, beat him!' it will go on beating until you tell it to stop. Now, off with you, and if you let that scoundrel rob you this time, never dare to come here again."

The boy thanked him very humbly, and rode off to the inn, where he went straight to his room as before. But the innkeeper had seen that handsome cane; his eyes glittered and he said to himself, "I will have that too." He waited until the house was quiet and then crept stealthily into the bedroom.

This time the boy had not gone to sleep. He had lain down with his eyes shut, clutching his cane in his hands, but what with hunger and what with anger he was very wide awake. The moment the innkeeper touched the cane the boy cried, "Beat him, beat him!"

The cane leaped from the bed and belabored the innkeeper on shoulders and back. Thwack, thwack, thwack, it went until the man was lying on the floor, howling for mercy. Then it began to break up the room. It smashed the window, it smashed the mirror, it smashed the table and the chair and the cupboard.

"Oh, stop it, stop it," wailed the innkeeper. "Make it stop, young sir, and I will give you back your donkey and your tablecloth."

"Stop!" cried the boy, "but do not leave him." And the cane hopped along behind the man until he came back with the magic donkey and the magic tablecloth.

The boy could not wait for morning. He spread the cloth on the bed and had a wonderful meal. He told the donkey to fill the nosebag with gold. Then he stuffed the ducats into one pocket and the tablecloth into the other, put the cane under his arm, climbed on the donkey, and trotted all the way home.

You can imagine how overjoyed his mother was to see him, and when he showed her what he had brought and told her the story of his adventures she was the happiest mother in all Tuscany.

from Tuscany

10

The Princess Who Couldn't Laugh

◦━━◆━━◦

THERE was once a King of Sicily who had only one child, a daughter whom he loved very much. She was the happiest child in the world, always gay and laughing, until her fifteenth birthday, when suddenly she fell silent. She hardly ever spoke and she never, never laughed or even smiled.

The King sent for his doctors, but none of them could cure the Princess. He called together all the wise men in his court, but no one could think how to make her laugh. The King grew so desperate that he sent his herald to proclaim from end to end of Sicily that if anyone could make the Princess laugh he should have her hand in marriage and inherit the kingdom. All kinds of people came to try their fortune, and they all failed.

Now, in the far south of Sicily there was a young shepherd who was driving his flock out to pasture one day when he stopped at a well to drink. There he saw a beautiful gold ring, set with diamonds, lying on the grass. He slipped the ring on his right hand, and immediately he began to sneeze and sneeze and sneeze, and he could not stop sneezing until he took off the ring. He slipped it on his left hand, and nothing happened.

"Oh," he said to himself, "this is a magic ring. I will go to the King's court to try my fortune and see if I can make the Princess laugh."

He drove his sheep back to the farm, said goodbye to the farmer, and set out to walk through the mountains and forests to Palermo. When night came on, he was following a path through a dark forest, and he said to himself, "The robbers come out at night. If they met me and took away my ring, I should be a ruined man. I must hide."

At that he climbed into a tall tree and tied himself to a branch with his belt and was soon fast asleep. But not for long. Loud voices wakened him, and looking down through the leaves, he saw thirteen robbers gathered round the foot of the tree.

74

They were saying what they had stolen during the day, and when the rest had finished, the leader of the band pulled three things out of his pocket and said, "These are the most valuable things of all. I took them from a monk. This tablecloth will serve a meal whenever you ask it to, and this purse will fill itself with gold coins whenever you want them, and if you play a tune on this pipe, everyone who hears it has to dance madly until you stop."

Then the robber chief spread out the tablecloth on the ground and cried, "Tablecloth, serve supper!"

Immediately plates and knives and forks and spoons came tumbling out of the air and arranged themselves neatly. A seven-branched silver candlestick sprang up in the middle, with all its candles burning brightly. Slices of white bread leaped on the plates, and thirteen bowls of steaming hot soup appeared beside them. The robbers fell to at once, and when they had finished their soup, the bowls vanished into air and in their places were plates piled high with macaroni, richly spiced and flavored, and flagons of red wine. By the time they had had their fill, they were all nearly asleep, and when everything but the table-cloth itself had disappeared, they settled down for the night among the dead leaves, the captain with the three magic things beside him.

75

The shepherd waited until they were all fast asleep and snoring. Then he climbed quietly down the tree, stuffed the tablecloth, the purse, and the pipe into his pocket, and tiptoed away through the forest until he found another tree in which to spend the night. Next morning the tablecloth gave him a splendid breakfast, and he set off for Palermo.

At the great door of the palace the gatekeeper barred his way, but the shepherd said, "I can make the Princess laugh," so they took him to the King.

The shepherd bowed very low. "Your Majesty," he said, "I can make the Princess laugh."

The King, who did not like the look of the shepherd in his ragged clothes, said, "Well, you may try," and took him into another room. Many lords and ladies of the court were there in all their finery, and at one end of the room, in a gilded chair under a scarlet canopy, sat the poor Princess, as sad and silent as ever.

"Your Majesty," said the shepherd, "if you will allow me to put this ring on your right hand—" He slipped it on the ring finger, and at once the King began to sneeze and sneeze and sneeze. He could not stop for a moment. He staggered about the room, sneezing and sneezing and sneezing, with his crown slipping over one eye. The courtiers tried to keep their faces straight, but the King looked too silly. First one began to laugh, then another, until they were all roaring with laughter, and in the end the Princess had to join in.

The shepherd whipped the ring off the King's hand. "Your Majesty," he said, "I have made the Princess laugh. I claim my reward."

"What!" roared the King. "You impertinent young good-for-nothing! You come here and make me look a fool in front of all my court, and then you expect to marry my daughter! I've half a mind to chop off your head! Guards, take him to the prison and lock him up for a year and a day. Perhaps that will teach him better manners."

The shepherd was marched away to the palace prison and locked up in a room with a dozen other prisoners. "Well," he said to himself, "if I can't marry the Princess, at least I needn't go hungry." He spread out his tablecloth on the floor and commanded it to serve a good dinner for them all. They fell to with a will, but just as they were finishing their soup, the guards looked through the grating in the prison door and saw what was going on. They dashed in and took the tablecloth and all the food.

"Well," said the shepherd, "if we can't eat, at least we can dance." He took out his pipe and began to play a merry tune, and at once all the prisoners took to dancing madly. They could not help it. Then the guards dashed in again, but they had to join in, and they made such a noise with their laughing and singing and stamping of feet that it echoed all through the palace.

"What is that dreadful noise?" said the King, who was still very cross. "Chamberlain, go and find out!"

You may be sure that the chamberlain went quickly, but as soon as he reached the prison he had to join in the dance and he could not get away.

The King fumed about his room until his patience gave out. "Captain of the Guard," he roared, "go and stop that noise!"

You may be sure that the captain went very quickly, but as soon as he reached the prison he too had to join in that mad dance, and the noise got louder and louder.

"There is nothing else for it," cried the King in a fury. "I must go myself!" So off he went, and as soon as he reached the prison he had to dance. But he knew what to do. He snatched the pipe from the shepherd and at once the dancing stopped.

The King was purple in the face with passion. As soon as he could speak, he said, "Guards, put this ras-

cal into a cell by himself and make sure that I never
see him or hear of him again."

As they carried the shepherd away, the magic purse
fell out of his pocket and the Chamberlain gave it to
the King. The shepherd had lost all his magic. He was
thrown into a little cell, and the door was locked and
bolted on him.

"Now what can I do?" he asked himself. "How
can I get out of here?" The walls and door were very
solid. There was a large window, but it had iron bars,
and when he tried to shake them they felt very strong.
It was getting dark and he was beginning to yawn, so
he lay down on the heap of straw in one corner to go
to sleep. He found himself lying on something hard.
He felt among the straw and discovered a long file.
You can guess how delighted he was. As soon as the
prison was silent and everyone seemed asleep, he set
to work very quietly to file through the window bars.
Just as the cocks began to crow, he scrambled through
the window, to find himself among the onions and
cabbages in the King's kitchen garden. He took to his
heels and ran for his life.

All day he walked on, getting very hungry and
wishing he still had the tablecloth, so when he reached
the edge of the forest he was delighted to see a large

fig tree covered with ripe fruit. It was a very odd tree, for all the figs growing on one side of it were black and all those on the other side were white, but he picked a handful of the black ones and sat down under the tree to eat them. Almost at once he had a very queer feeling in his head. He put up his hand and found that two large horns were growing out of his forehead! He sprang to his feet in horror. What was he to do? Then the white figs caught his eye. He ate one, and one of the horns vanished. He felt for it carefully. Yes, it had gone! He ate another white fig and the second horn went to look for the first. Then he climbed into a nearby tree, fastened himself to a branch with his belt, and was soon fast asleep.

Next morning the shepherd made a good breakfast of white figs. Then he filled one of his pockets with them and filled the other with black figs, and set off for Palermo.

When he reached the city, he bought a red cloak to cover his green tunic and a red hood which hid most of his face, so that the King's guards should not know him. Next he bought a little basket, in which he laid six of the finest black figs on a cushion of straw, and he took up his stand near the great gate of the palace.

Soon he saw the King's steward returning from the market.

"Sir steward," he cried, "see what fine figs I have for sale. Figs fit for a King! All for one ducat!"

"Indeed," said the steward, "they are very fine. I have never seen such fine black figs in my life, and the King and Princess are very fond of figs. I will buy them."

When the King and the Princess finished their dinner of quail, venison, sweet red wine, and gilded gingerbread, the steward set the black figs before them in a golden dish. "What wonderful figs!" said the Princess, smiling. "Thank you, Master Steward." In no time she and the King had eaten the six plump black fruit, and a few minutes later they sat staring at each other in horror. Long horns had grown out of their heads!

"Steward!" roared the King, and the poor man came forward, pale and trembling. "Where did you get these figs?"

"From a peddler, Your Majesty," he stammered. "A peddler by the palace gate."

"Bring him here at once," roared the King, "or I'll chop off your head!"

In a few minutes the steward came back with the shepherd, to find the Princess crying and the King still furious, which was natural enough.

"You scoundrel!" cried the King. "See what you've

done with your black-magic figs! If you don't take off these horns, I'll chop off your head!"

The shepherd bowed low, still keeping his hood close to hide his face. "If Your Majesty will eat this white fig—" he said.

The King snorted, but he gobbled it up, and almost at once one of his horns disappeared. The Princess clapped her hands, and the King almost smiled.

The shepherd flung back his hood. "I am the man," he said, "who made the Princess laugh." He smiled at her and she smiled at him. He was really, she thought, a very good-looking young man. "I have enough white figs to remove the other three horns, but I will give them to you only if you first give me back my tablecloth, purse, and pipe, and let me marry the Princess."

"We'll soon see about that!" bellowed the King, who was now almost beside himself with rage. "Guards! Search him and give me the white figs."

Three of the guards stepped forward, but the shepherd lifted his hand and looked fiercely at the King.

"Sire," he said, "if the figs are taken from me by force, they will lose all their magic, and nothing I can do will bring it back. You can chop off my head, but you and the Princess will have to wear horns all the rest of your lives."

How brave and handsome he is, thought the Princess. She clung to the King's arm and sobbed, "Oh, please, Papa, do what he asks. I couldn't bear to have these horns all the rest of my life."

It was all too much for the King. He swallowed his rage as best he could, and sent the chamberlain to get the shepherd's property from the royal treasury. As soon as the tablecloth, the purse, and the pipe were in his hands, the shepherd laid another white fig before the King. No sooner had he eaten it than his horn disappeared.

"Now," he said, "figs for the Princess!"

The shepherd smiled at him and smiled very sweetly at the Princess.

"She shall have them," he answered, "as soon as we are married."

A priest was sent for, and he married them then and there. Then the Princess ate her two white figs, and at once her horns disappeared, leaving her as beautiful as she had always been.

The shepherd-prince spread his tablecloth on the royal table and commanded it to provide the most splendid wedding feast that Sicily had ever seen, and the rejoicings went on for seven days and seven nights.

They always had all the money they wanted, for the purse filled itself up with golden ducats whenever they needed them. The feasts they gave were famous far and wide, and with his magic pipe the Prince taught all their children to dance. Never again did the Princess forget how to laugh.

from Sicily

11

The Snake under the Stone

THERE was once a man who went into the forest to gather firewood, and he had not gone far before he came upon a snake lying under a large stone.

"Help me!" said the snake. "This stone has rolled on me and I can't get away. I shall starve."

The man was sorry for the snake, so he raised the stone a little with his axe and the snake crawled out.

"Now," said the snake, "I am so hungry that I am going to eat you."

"No," cried the man, "that can't be right, because I have just done you a good turn." But the snake would not agree.

"Well, let us find someone else and ask him. If he says it is right, you can eat me."

They went on together along the road until they came to a horse tied to an oak tree. It had eaten every leaf within reach, and it was as thin as a stick.

"Horse," said the snake, "is it right for me to eat this man who has just saved my life?"

"Certainly," the horse answered. "Look at me. I was one of the finest horses in the world. I carried my master faithfully for many years, and now that I am too old and weak to carry him any longer he has tied me to this oak and left me to starve. So eat up the man, snake. That is the proper thing to do."

"This horse is not a fair judge," said the man. "Let us find someone else." He set the horse free and it began to eat the grass by the roadside.

The man and the snake went on together along the road until they came to a mulberry tree, whose leaves were full of holes.

"Mulberry tree," said the snake, "is it right for me to eat this man who has just saved my life?"

"Yes," the tree answered. "Look at me. I have given my master so many leaves that he has bred the finest silkworms in the world. But now that I'm too old even to stand up straight, he says he is going to cut me down and throw me into the fire. So eat the man. That seems to be the proper way to behave."

"This tree is not a good judge," said the man. "Let us find someone else." He propped up the tree carefully with two long sticks.

The man and the snake went on together along the road until they met a fox.

"Fox," said the snake, "is it right for me to eat this man who has just saved my life?"

"No," said the fox, "I don't think it is. But show me just what the man did."

So they all went back along the road until they came to the stone. Then the snake stretched itself out beside the road, and the man and the fox rolled the stone on top of it, so that it could not move.

"Now, snake," said the man, "you can stay there."

And the man and the fox went away together.

from Piedmont

12

A Monkey in the House

ONE day when the lawyer Signor Silvio came back from the law courts, he found his little house just as he had left it in the morning. His bed had not been made, the dishes hadn't been washed, nothing had been swept or dusted, and there was no sign of Gobbi, his servant boy, who was supposed to look after the house.

Silvio was angry, as well he might be.

"Gobbi!" he called.

There was no answer.

"Where is that lazy young knave?" he asked himself. "Gobbi! Gobbi!"

Still there was no answer. Silvio went all over the house, but he could not find Gobbi.

"Fast asleep somewhere, I expect," he muttered. "Why do I go on paying him good wages for doing nothing? I've warned him often enough. Now I really will get rid of him. It's lucky I had my dinner at the tavern. I wouldn't have got anything here."

The sun was hot and it was time for his usual afternoon rest, his siesta. He made himself comfortable on a long couch, but hardly had he lain down when he heard the door opening. As he looked, a funny little face came round the edge of the door. It was followed by a black furry body and a long black furry tail. It was a monkey.

"Well!" exclaimed Silvio. "What do you want?"

The monkey came across the room, bowed to him, and shook hands with itself. Then it turned a somersault backward and stood there, grinning.

"You're a very nice little monkey," said Silvio, "but you can't stay here. You must go back to your owner."

The monkey shook its head.

"Oh, yes, you must." He took the monkey by the paw, led it out of the room, and firmly shut the door. Then he lay down again.

A few minutes later there was a scuffling noise

under his window, and the monkey jumped on the windowsill and came bounding into the room. It stood and grinned at him.

"No," said Silvio, "you've got to go home."

The monkey looked very sad, but Silvio picked it up, dropped it gently into the garden, and shut the window.

Silvio had just settled down to the book he was reading when there came a gentle tap-tap at the door. He took no notice. Tap, tap, tap, tap . . . it went on. Silvio was getting cross, but when he opened the door there was the monkey grinning at him so comically that he could not help himself, he had to burst out laughing.

The monkey ran into the room, sprang to a chair, and stood on its hands on the chair back, waving his legs and tail in the air. It looked so funny that Silvio had to go on laughing. It did a dozen tricks like this and then curled up on a rug and went fast asleep.

When it was time for Silvio to go back to the law courts, he looked at the sleeping monkey and made up his mind to leave it there. When he came back, he had the surprise of his life. The table had been cleared, his bed had been made, all the floors had been swept, every piece of furniture had been polished until it shone, and in the kitchen he found a large pot of spaghetti bubbling on the stove. The monkey was stirring it.

"Did you do all this?" he asked.

The monkey nodded and grinned.

"Do you want to stay and look after me, then?"

The monkey nodded and nodded and nodded until it looked as though its head would fall off.

So that was settled, and when Gobbi came in very late the next morning, yawning and rubbing his eyes as usual, Silvio boxed his ears and told him he wasn't wanted any more.

The monkey went on keeping house, and Silvio had never been so well looked after in his life before. Then one day he met his old friend Filippo in the tavern, and told him all about the monkey.

Filippo frowned. "This is very strange," he said. "Surely no monkey would do all this. You know, Silvio, that I have read much in books of magic. Will you let me come and see your monkey?"

"Willingly," replied Silvio, and took him at once to the house, where they found the monkey sweeping out the bedroom.

Filippo spoke three strange words. The monkey threw down the broom, stood up straight, and looked at him. Filippo raised both hands and spoke great words of power.

There was a blinding flash, like lightning, and the room filled with smoke, which drifted out slowly through the window. Then they saw that the monkey had vanished and in its place stood a young man.

"I thank you with all my heart," he said, bowing low to them both. "I was turned into a monkey by a wicked old witch because I would not work in her house. But if you will have me, Signor Silvio, I will work in your house for as long as you wish."

"Have you!" cried Silvio. "Indeed I will. Nothing could please me more." And the young man looked after him even better than the monkey had done.

from Rome

13

The Buried Treasure

YEARS ago there was a Prince in Sicily who was very poor because the King his father had spent nearly everything they had. One day an old man came to the Prince and said, "Your Highness, there is a great treasure buried somewhere in this kingdom."

"How do you know?" asked the Prince.

"Because my father told me. He saw a magician burying the treasure—sacks and barrels full of gold coins, great chests that were bursting with diamonds and rubies, sapphires and emeralds, and long necklaces of pearls."

"Oh, if only I could find it," cried the Prince. "Where is it buried?"

"That I cannot tell you," answered the old man, shaking his head. "My father would never tell me, or go near the place again, because he was so afraid of the magician. By magic it was buried, and only by magic can it be found."

So the Prince set to work to study magic. There were many books of magic in Sicily in those days, and he read them all. In the very last book he found a spell for discovering buried treasure.

No sooner had he spoken the words of power than an invisible hand took hold of his hand and led him across the country, for mile after mile, until he came to the bank of a river in which there was an island. The hand lifted his arm to point to the island and then it was gone.

The Prince found a little boat in which he rowed himself across, and the moment he stepped ashore on the island a magician appeared—a tall, fierce-looking old man with gray hair and beard who wore a long black robe covered with mysterious signs.

"By your strong magic you have found the treasure," said the magician, "but it is still guarded by magic. There is only one way in which you can dig it up. You must set ten million ants to dig for it."

"But there can't be ten million ants in this small island!" said the Prince.

"You must call together all the ants in Sicily," replied the magician, "and when they reach the river bank, you must send them across two at a time, one to paddle and one to steer, in half a walnut shell. This is the only way." And with these words he vanished into air.

There was nothing else to do. By a spell from his book of magic, the Prince summoned the ants, until the earth was black with them.

He found half a walnut shell and put it into the river. Two ants crawled into it and paddled across, and the shell floated back.

Then two more ants went across.

Then two more ants went across.

Then two more ants went across.

Then two more ants went across.

Then two more ants went across. . . .

When the ten million ants have all crossed the river, I will tell you the rest of the story.

from Sicily

14

The Turkish Slave

In Istria there was a merchant who had an only son named Fairbrow. When he had left school, his father said to him, "My son, you are old enough to go out and see the world and learn how to trade. I will give you one of my ships and six thousand gold ducats so that you can buy goods in foreign lands and bring them home and sell them. You must make sure you buy things that you can sell at a profit."

Fairbrow sailed away and soon reached the harbor of a large city. He went ashore to look for goods that he could sell in Istria. He came to a place where a dead man lay on a table. A woman beside him sobbed bitterly.

"What is the matter?" asked Fairbrow.

"This is my husband," she answered. "He died yesterday. He owed money to many people and they will not let him be buried until all his debts are paid. But I have no money." And she began to weep again.

"This is very wrong," said Fairbrow. "The dead cannot rest until they are properly buried. If you will tell all his creditors to come to me, I will pay his debts."

The poor widow thanked him gratefully and went away to find the creditors. Presently they came hurrying, with their bills in their hands, and Fairbrow paid them all. Then he had only three ducats left, and there was nothing to do but go back home. So he sailed for Istria.

"You have come back very quickly," said his father. "What goods have you bought?"

Fairbrow was so afraid to tell the truth that he told his father a wicked lie. "No sooner had we put out to sea," he answered, "than we were captured by Turkish pirates, who said they would kill me if I did not give them all my money. I gave them the six thousand ducats and they let me go, and here I am."

"Thank heaven they did not kill you," said his father. "Now you must try again. I will give you another six thousand ducats and this time you shall have my finest ship, which carries so many guns and soldiers that no pirate will dare to attack you."

Once again Fairbrow put out to sea, and when they had sailed for seven days and seven nights into the East they saw a large ship flying the Turkish flag. She sailed swiftly toward them but showed no signs of getting ready to attack.

"The Turks have counted our guns," said Fairbrow. "They want to trade, not to fight."

When the two ships were close enough, he hailed the Turkish captain, asking him whether he would like to come aboard.

The captain answered in Italian that he would, and he clambered on the deck. He was a big man with a bushy black beard and a green turban, and he was followed by six sailors, bringing a girl who was veiled from head to foot.

"Where do you come from?" asked Fairbrow.

"From Turkey," replied the captain.

"Have you anything to sell?"

"Very precious goods," replied the captain. "This maiden. We carried her off from the palace. She is the Sultan's daughter."

So saying, he lifted her veil, and Fairbrow was amazed. He had never seen anyone half so beautiful, and in that instant he fell madly in love with her.

As soon as he could speak, he said, "How much do you want for her?"

"Six thousand golden ducats," answered the Turk.

"I will have her!" cried Fairbrow. He sent two men down to his cabin for the bags of gold, and when they had been counted out on one of the hatches, the Turks rowed back to their ship.

Fairbrow led the beautiful Princess to his cabin. She was very frightened, but he was kind and gentle. He handed her over to the priest who was on board, to be taught Christianity and some Italian. He visited her every day, falling more and more deeply in love with her, and before the ship reached home he persuaded her to marry him.

He went alone to find his father, who made him very welcome and soon said, "Well, my son, I hope you have had better luck than on your first voyage. What merchandise have you brought home?"

"The most beautiful girl you have ever seen," answered Fairbrow, "the Sultan of Turkey's daughter. I paid six thousand ducats for her and I have married her."

The merchant was furious. "You miserable knave!" he cried. "Are you mad? Six thousand ducats for a slave girl? Get out of my sight! I never want to see you again!" And he drove the young man out into the street.

Fairbrow had no money and nowhere to go, but presently he found a small room for the Princess and himself in a nearby town.

"How are we to live?" cried Fairbrow in despair. "I don't know any way of earning my living and I haven't a single ducat to my name!"

"I can paint pictures," said the Princess, "and you can take them into the city and sell them, but you must *never* tell anyone they are painted by me."

They found a shop that would trust them with brushes, paints, and canvas, and the Princess set to work with a will, for by this time she loved her handsome husband as much as he loved her.

All went well at first. The pictures were so beautiful that when Fairbrow showed them in the market square people gladly paid twenty ducats or more for one. Very soon he and the Princess were quite well off. Then one day a party of Turks, disguised as Italians, came into the square. They had been sent out by the Sultan to search for his daughter far and wide. As soon as they saw the pictures, they knew she must have painted them.

"How much are the pictures?" they asked.

"Twenty-five ducats each," replied Fairbrow.

"We will buy them all," said the Turk, "and we should like more. Where can we get them?"

Fairbrow was so pleased that he forgot the Princess's warning. "My wife paints them," he said. "If you will come home with me, you can buy as many as you like."

Off they went to the house, and the Turks seized the Princess, although she wept bitterly, and carried her off to their ship, which at once set sail for Turkey.

The Sultan was overjoyed to see his daughter, and to make sure she was not stolen again he shut her up in a tall tower in the palace gardens. It had only one door, which was never unlocked except when the Sultan went to see her or servants took in food. There she lived sadly with her maidens, for she missed her husband very much.

Fairbrow too was miserable. He had lost his beautiful wife, and very soon he had no money left. Day after day he wandered through the city docks, looking in vain for a ship that was going to Turkey. Then he began to wander along the seashore, still hoping to find a ship.

One day he found a poor old fisherman trying to launch his boat, which was stuck fast in the sand.

Fairbrow went to his help and together they got the boat into the sea.

"Thank you, sir," said the fisherman. "Thank you. I am getting too old to manage the boat alone."

"Then may I come fishing with you?" asked Fairbrow, and the man was very glad to have him.

As soon as they had caught some large fish, the man cooked the best of them on a little charcoal stove in the boat, and they made a good meal, for they were both very hungry. Then they lay down to rest in the bottom of the boat. The sea was calm, the sun was warm, and they soon fell fast asleep. They slept until a great wave crashed into the boat, soaking them to the skin. They sprang to their feet, to find that a gale was blowing, driving the boat away from the shore. No matter how hard they rowed, the wind was too strong for them.

All night the boat was driven eastward. Next morning a Turkish ship appeared and carried them both off to Turkey, where they were sold as slaves in the marketplace. You can guess how miserable they were. They thought they would be beaten and half starved.

Their master was the Sultan's chief gardener, however, and he was not cruel to them so long as they worked hard. They were set to look after all the rose beds in the palace gardens, and before long they were working near the tower.

The Princess's balcony overlooked the garden, and her maidens used to get flowers for her every day from the gardeners. They had made a long rope by tying their silken girdles together, and they lowered a great basket, which the gardeners filled with the finest blooms they could find. Fairbrow did not know who was in the tower, and he was astonished and overjoyed one day, when he was filling the basket, to hear the Princess's voice from the room at the top of the tower. As soon as he had got his breath back, he began to sing a love song that he had often sung to her in Italy. She knew his voice at once. With a wild cry she ran to the balcony and there she saw Fairbrow in the garden below, looking up at her.

"My love!" she cried. "Get into the basket and cover yourself with the flowers." Then she called all her maidens and together they pulled at the silken rope. Even the Princess lent a hand. In a few moments Fairbrow leaped out of the basket onto the balcony and took her in his arms.

How happy they were to be together again! Every day after that, Fairbrow visited his wife in the tower, and the old man kept watch to warn them if the head gardener was coming. Soon they were planning to escape. The Princess had a great number of diamonds, pearls, emeralds, and rubies, besides chains, bracelets, and anklets of the finest gold. Filling his pockets with jewels, Fairbrow went to the harbor night after night when he was supposed to be asleep, until he found an Italian ship. He went aboard and offered the captain a handful of jewels to take him and his companions home to Italy, which he gladly said he would do.

That night, when all the palace was asleep, Fairbrow crept silently from the hut where he slept on the floor with the other garden slaves, and went to the tower. The maidens lowered the Princess to the ground, then they let down three baskets full of gold and precious stones, and last they climbed down the silken rope themselves. They stole through the darkness to the harbor, and presently the ship was ready to set out to sea.

Then a terrible thought came to Fairbrow. In his haste and joy he had entirely forgotten the old man. "I must go back," he said to the Princess. "We were friends. I cannot leave him to live all the rest of his life as a miserable slave. I must go back for him."

At first the captain refused to go. It was too dangerous, he said. If anyone discovered that the Princess had run away, the Sultan's guards would be searching the harbor. When the Princess gave him a pearl necklace worth thousands of ducats, he agreed to go back.

Once again Fairbrow crept silently through the shadows of the palace garden and into the hut. The old fisherman was fast asleep, so Fairbrow whispered into his ear until he awoke. They stole away together and shortly the ship was carrying them safely out of the harbor. By the time the sun rose, they had left Turkey far behind.

When they reached Fairbrow's native city, they bought a beautiful house where they could live happily together. They asked Fairbrow's father to come and live with them and he came gladly, for he had really been very sorry to lose his only son.

Fairbrow gave a great feast for all his neighbors, and when it was over, he said to the fisherman, "Now, old friend, you and I have always helped each other. I am going to share all my riches with you. You shall have half our treasure."

"I thank you with all my heart," answered the old man, "but I am not what I seem. I am the spirit of the man whose debts you paid, and all your good fortune has come to you because you did that and because you were so kind to the Princess when you bought her as a slave. Then you risked your life to bring me home.

You have deserved all your happiness." And with these words he vanished.

from Istria

15

The Silliest Man in Italy

PERUONTO was the ugliest, laziest, silliest young man in the whole of Italy, and his mother, who was a poor widow, did not know what to do with him. She would scream at him until she was hoarse, and still he would do nothing for her.

One day they had no wood left for their fire and she asked Peruonto to go to the forest and get some more. But would he go? Not he. All he would do was to lie in the shade and sleep and snore. But when they had had nothing to eat all day, even Peruonto began to think that something would have to be done. He was getting very hungry. Next morning early he said he would go to the forest.

"You won't get anything to eat until you do," said his mother. "Here is your axe. Don't lose it, and don't lose yourself, and if you want any dinner bring home a good bundle of firewood."

Off he went, very slowly, walking as usual as though he were walking on eggs. As he went, he counted his steps up to ten, which was as far as he could count, and then started again at one.

At last he came to the forest, and there beside a little stream he found three pretty girls lying fast asleep in the sunshine, with a log for a pillow. They were so very pretty that even Peruonto had to stop and stare, and he had just enough sense to see that if they went on sleeping there when the sun was high they would get badly sunburned. Perhaps hunger had sharpened his wits. He tiptoed clumsily into the forest and cut down some leafy boughs and stuck them into the ground to shade the girls from the sun.

Hardly had he finished when they opened their eyes and saw him. No, they didn't fall in love with him. He was much too ugly and dirty for any girl to do that. But when they saw how kind he had been, they agreed to reward him. which was easy for them, for they were fairies.

"Thank you, young man," said the oldest. "Because you have done this for us, we will give you a magic

112

present. We give you the power to wish, and anything you wish will happen."

At that they vanished, leaving Peruonto gaping like an idiot. He tried to think of something to wish, but he was too stupid, so after a while he went into the forest. He cut down so many boughs that when he had tied them into a faggot with a wild vine he could not lift it.

"Ouch," he said, and sat down heavily on it. "I can't carry this home. I wish it would carry me."

At once the faggot stood up on invisible legs and trotted away like a pony. Peruonto held tight, too stupid to be frightened. He hadn't told the faggot where to go, and very soon it was trotting through the streets of the town. You can guess how astonished the people were, and how the children ran after him, shouting and screaming.

Very soon they were passing the King's palace, making such a noise that the Princess came out on her balcony to see what it was all about. Peruonto looked so comic, riding his faggot, that she burst out laughing. Peruonto heard her. He looked up, and he was very angry.

"I wish you were my wife," he cried. "I'd soon teach you to laugh at me."

The Princess could not help herself. She lifted her

beautiful dress, ran down the stairs, ran into the street, and ran so fast after Peruonto that soon she had caught up to him and climbed on the faggot behind him.

Away they went, right through the town, leaving the crowd behind, and presently they came to a little church by the roadside.

"Stop the faggot," cried the Princess. "We must get married here." Peruonto told it to stop and they went into the church, where the Princess commanded the priest to marry them. She hated the sight of Peruonto, but she could not help herself. She was bewitched.

"Now tell the faggot to take us to your home," she said.

Off they went again, faster than before. The Princess was horrified when she saw that miserable, tumbledown cottage, but she took Peruonto inside and said to his mother, "We've come to live here." The poor widow was too frightened to say a word. All she could do was set to work and boil the beans for supper.

Meanwhile the King stormed about his palace and the Queen wept and the royal guards were searching everywhere for the Princess. Next day they found her in the cottage and took her and her husband to the King.

"What!" he roared, when he had heard the story.

"You have married this dolt, this simpleton, this raga-muffin with the brains of a sheep, this dirty scarecrow dressed in dirty rags! What do you mean by it? How dare you?"

Peruonto gaped and the Princess burst into tears. "I couldn't help it," she sobbed. "I had to."

"You had to!" roared the King. "Stuff and non-sense! Balderdash! You're a shameless hussy! You're a disgrace! You're not fit to live! Guards, take the Princess, take this dirty creature, nail them up in a barrel and throw it into the sea!"

In vain the Princess and the Queen wept and begged, while Peruonto stood and gaped. It was no use. The King was beside himself. Very soon Peruonto and the Princess were nailed up in a great barrel and thrown into the sea.

There were only two good things about it. The barrel floated, and one of the Princess's maids managed to give her some raisins and dried figs for them to eat.

The barrel sailed away before the wind, while the Princess cried her eyes out and Peruonto could think of nothing to say. Presently the Princess recovered enough to say, "Have you no magic wishes left? Can you not save us?"

"Give me some figs and raisins," Peruonto grunted.

She gave him a handful, and when he had eaten them, he said, "What do you want me to wish?"

"You dolt!" she cried, for she hated him more than ever. "Wish this barrel to turn into a fine ship that will carry us safely to land."

"Give me some figs and raisins," he said, and when he had eaten them, he wished.

In a moment they found themselves on the deck of a ship, as fine as you could wish to see. All the white sails were set, all the seamen were busy about the deck, the wind was fair, and before the sun had set they reached land, where there was not a house or a human being in sight.

"What do we do now?" asked Peruonto.

"You wish us on land, and you wish the ship turned into a splendid palace."

"Give me some raisins and figs," he said, and when he had eaten them, he wished.

They found themselves on the shore, looking out to sea. The ship had vanished. They heard a sound like thunder behind them, and when they turned round, there was a splendid palace, surrounded by beautiful gardens. They went inside and servants in rich liveries bowed to them and asked their commands. Here was everything they could wish, but when the Princess looked at her husband, she found she could not bear the sight of him. He looked dirtier, more stupid than ever.

Then she saw what to do. "Wish yourself good-looking, sensible, clever, and beautifully dressed," she said. "Make yourself into a prince."

In a trice he did it, without waiting for figs and raisins. He was transformed, and the Princess was so overjoyed that she threw herself into his arms.

They were happy, and time passed. Presently twins were born to them, two beautiful boys, and their happiness was complete. But the Princess began wishing she could see her mother again, and her father too, although he had been so cruel to her.

Peruonto was much too sensible now not to know at once what to do. He wished for the King to come and see them.

Next day the King went hunting with his courtiers, and he rode faster and farther than he had ever done before. He did not know why. Presently all the others were left far behind and he found himself in a part of the country he had never seen before. There was not a house in sight, except for a beautiful palace overlooking the sea. This he felt he must visit, he did not know why, so he rode up to the great door, which was wide open. There was no one in sight. He walked into the fine marble hall. Then two beautiful little boys appeared, dressed like princelings.

"Grandfather!" they cried, and hugged his knees. He could only stare and gasp. Then the Princess appeared, leading Peruonto, who looked every inch a prince. "This is my husband," she said.

The King was so astonished that at first he could not say a word. Then he begged them to forgive him, which they did very gladly, and they sat down to a wonderful feast that was served by invisible hands while invisible musicians played the sweetest music. The children were allowed to eat as much as they liked.

Then they all went back to the King's palace, where the Queen laughed and cried, she was so glad to see them. Peruonto wished for his poor mother everything that he wished for himself, and they all lived in great happiness.

from Naples